↠ A FABER PICTURE BOOK ↞

Once Upon a Snowstorm

RICHARD JOHNSON

First published in the UK in 2018
First published in the USA in 2018
by Faber and Faber Limited
Bloomsbury House, 74–77 Great Russell Street, London WC1B 3DA
Text and illustration © Richard Johnson, 2018
HB ISBN 978–0–571–33928–0
PB ISBN 978–0–571–33929–7
All rights reserved.
Printed in China
10 9 8 7 6 5 4 3 2 1
The moral rights of Richard Johnson have been asserted.
A CIP record for this book is available from the British Library.

FABER & FABER

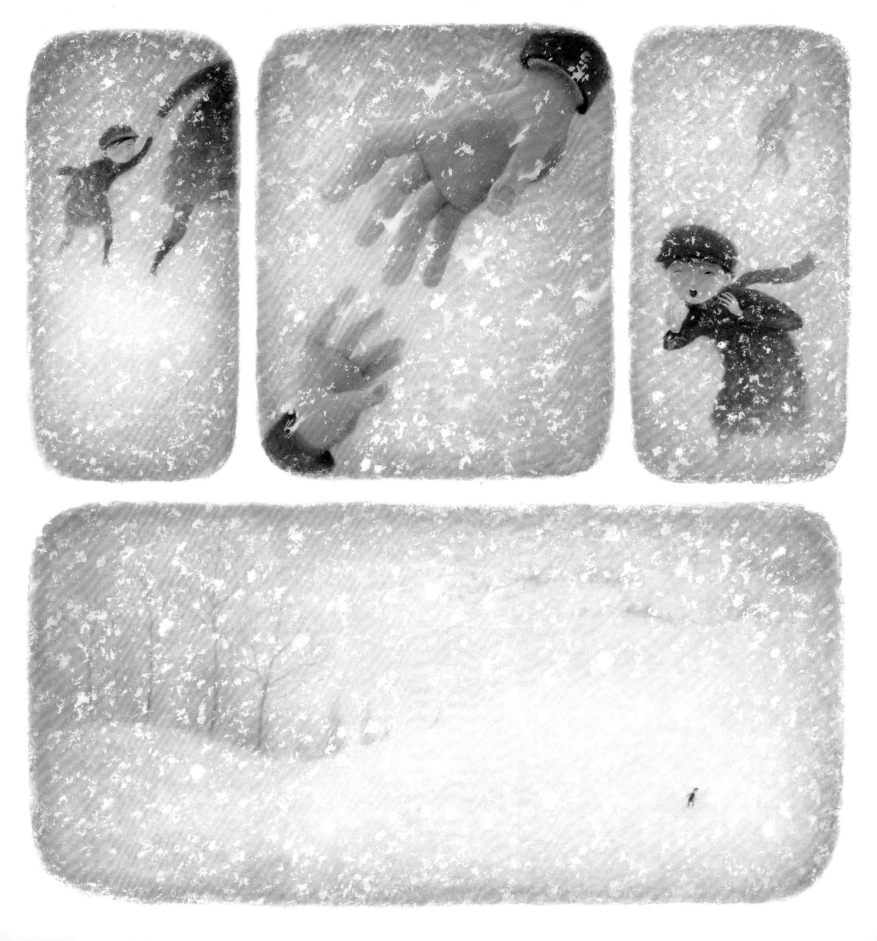

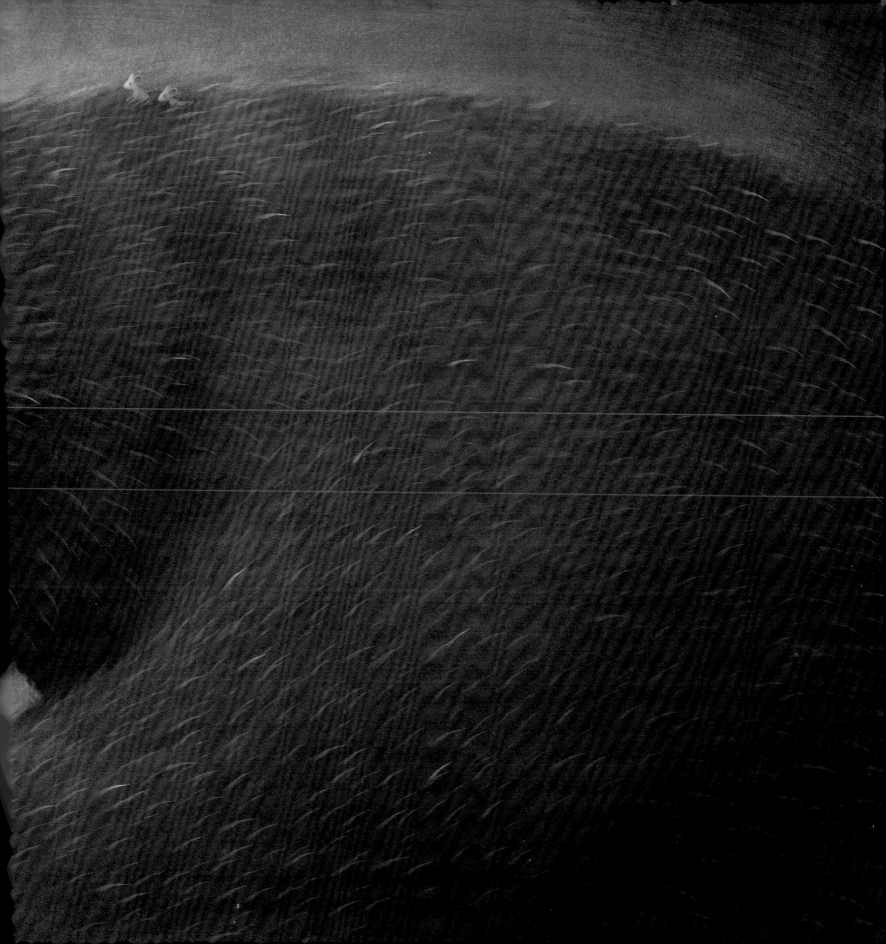